OTHER YEARLING BOOKS YOU WILL ENJOY:

YEARLING BOOKS/YOUNG YEARLINGS/YEARLING CLASSICS are
designed especially to entertain and enlighten young people.
Patricia Reilly Giff, consultant to this series, received the bach-
elor's degree from Marymount College. She holds the master's
degree in history from St. John's University, and a Professional
Diploma in Reading from Hofstra University. She was a teacher
and reading consultant for many years, and is the author of
numerous books for young readers.

For a complete listing of all Yearling titles,
write to Dell Readers Service,
P.O. Box 1045, South Holland, IL 60473.

D1366406

F. N. MONJO

Grand Papa and Ellen Aroon

Being an Account of Some of the Happy Times
Spent Together by Thomas Jefferson and His
Favorite Granddaughter

illustrated by Richard Cuffari

A Yearling Book

Published by
Dell Publishing
a division of
Bantam Doubleday Dell Publishing Group, Inc.
666 Fifth Avenue
New York, New York 10103

for Nick and Livvie

ISBN: 0-440-43004-6

Reprinted by arrangement with Henry Holt and Company, Inc.

Printed in the United States of America

One Previous Edition

March 1990

10 9 8 7 6 5 4 3 2 1

CWO

Contents

❧1❧

Mr. Mammoth

There's so much to tell you about Grand Papa, I don't know where to begin. My real name is Ellen. But five years ago, when I was a *little* girl, only four years old, Sister Anne started calling me "Eleanora"—to be fancy, I reckon. I couldn't say Eleanora. All I could say was "Ellen Aroon."

Well, Grand Papa took it up, and now that's what he's called me ever since. "Ellen Aroon! I'll catch you in bed yet, one of these mornings. You see if I don't, Ellen Aroon!"

Sister Anne's a whole lot older than I am. She's fourteen. I'm only nine. She must be jealous because I have a nickname and she doesn't.

Yesterday she said to me, "Ellen, I believe

I'll change my name. I'm going to call myself Anastasia, instead of plain old Anne!"

Did you ever hear of anything so silly in your whole life? Anastasia, my foot! Isn't that just like Sister Anne?

Mama says we children are enough to run her crazy. Besides Mama and Papa, there's the six of us—five girls and my brother, Jeff. First comes Sister Anne; then Jeff; then me; then Cornelia; then Virginia; then Mary. She's only two.

Sometimes Aunt Polly's and Uncle Jack's children come to stay with us, too. Their names are Francis and Maria. They're my first cousins. Aunt Polly was Mama's sister. She was so sweet and pretty. But poor little Aunt Polly died last spring.

Mama writes to Papa and to Grand Papa almost every week. Mama tells them which one of us has gotten over measles, or mumps, or whooping cough.

Here's what Grand Papa calls Mama: "My dear Patsy." Here's what Mama calls Papa: "Mr. Randolph!"

My Papa's in Congress in Washington City. So's my Uncle Jack, Aunt Polly's husband. Grand Papa is in Washington City, too. But *he*

lives in the President's House on Pennsylvania Avenue, because he is President of the United States.

Mama says Grand Papa has lots of friends. They call themselves "republicans." They call Grand Papa "Mr. President," or sometimes, "Mr. Jefferson."

Mama says Grand Papa has quite a few enemies, too. Their real name is Federalists. We call them "the Feds."

You know what the Feds call Grand Papa? Sometimes they call him a Jacobin. Mama says a Jacobin was the worst kind of Frenchman—the kind that was always sending somebody away to have his head chopped off in the French Revolution. So I don't see why the Feds call Grand Papa a Jacobin. *He* never had anybody's head chopped off, not in his whole life.

You know what else the Feds call him? They call him "Mad Tom." Mama says the Feds must think Grand Papa's crazy, to call him that. But I say the *Feds* must be crazy themselves, if that's what they think of Grand Papa. Grand Papa's the smartest man I ever knew!

The Feds call him something else, too. They call him "Mr. Mammoth!" You know why? Because Grand Papa collects old fossil bones of dinosaurs, and mastodons, and woolly mammoths. He's a scientist.

"A natural historian," Mama says. But I guess the Feds think he's kind of peculiar to like fossils.

"That's politics," says Mama. But Mr. Mammoth doesn't say anything at all about the Feds. Isn't that just like Grand Papa?

Mama says I must *never* call Grand Papa a Jacobin, or Mad Tom, or Mr. Mammoth. It might hurt his feelings.

While Papa and Grand Papa are away in Washington City, we live with Mama on our farm in Virginia. It's a pretty place called Edgehill. Mama teaches all of us our lessons, except for Jeff. He goes to Latin school in town. He walks there by himself. Mama teaches us English, and French, and history.

Grand Papa writes lots of letters to all of us children, too. Here's what Grand Papa calls Jeff: "My dear Jefferson." Here's something Grand Papa wrote to Sister Anne: "How does Jefferson get on with his French? Will he let Ellen catch him?"

I *may* catch him at that, because Jeff likes hunting a heap more than French or Latin. Jeff would rather take his gun and go off hunting

quail, or pheasant, or turkey. Sometimes he goes barefoot, wading icy creeks, tramping through the snow. Jeff doesn't mind the cold a bit.

Mama says Jeff's going to be just as tall as Grand Papa someday. Grand Papa's six feet two.

Grand Papa loves writing letters. He loves to receive letters from us, too. I never know just what to say in my letters to *him*. Grand Papa tells us to write about all the little things that are happening here at Edgehill.

"You have a thousand little things to tell me," says Grand Papa, "which I am fond to hear. For instance, the health of everybody, and particularly of your dear Mama; how many Bantam chicks you have raised; how often you and Anne have rode to Monticello to see if the tulips are safe."

And Grand Papa asks us about our studies. He sends us poems he cuts out of the paper, and tells us to paste them in our scrapbooks. And he sends Jeff pictures of soldiers and birds and Indians.

When Grand Papa writes to Mama, he says, "Present me affectionately in kisses to all the dear children."

Mama says, when I was a very little girl, Grand Papa would write and tell her to give me some gingerbread as a present from him, so I wouldn't *forget* him. Imagine anybody forgetting Grand Papa!

Mama says I used to call him "my seet Grand Papa," when I was a little girl, and couldn't even say "sweet" right.

Here's something else Grand Papa does: he checks up on you! He keeps a count of the letters he writes to you, and of the letters you write to him. And if you don't write as many to *him* as he writes to *you*, he says you're in *debt* to him.

Grand Papa wrote me just such a letter in May, saying I'd written him only one letter since January. Then he said: "Balance due from E.W. Randolph to Th. J.—Letters, 4." (E.W. Randolph—that's *me*, Ellen Wayles Randolph, Ellen Aroon. Th. J.—Thomas Jefferson—that's Grand Papa.)

And Grand Papa added: "So stands the account for this year, my dear Ellen, between you and me. Unless it be soon paid off, I shall send the sheriff after you."

Here's another letter Grand Papa sent to us. It's a poem, sort of; a puzzle he learned when he was just a little boy, himself. Grand Papa wrote:

"The four lines which I now enclose you will be a good lesson on minding your stops in writing. I allow you a day to find out yourself how to read these lines so as to make them true. . . ."

Here are the four lines:

I've seen the sea all in a blaze of fire
I've seen a house high as the moon and higher
I've seen the sun at twelve o'clock at night
I've seen the man who saw this wondrous sight

I beat Jeff and Sister Anne with the answer. Can you make it read right? Give up? Stick some commas and periods in, and try it this way:

I've seen the sea. All in a blaze of fire,
I've seen a house. High as the moon, and higher,
I've seen the sun. At twelve o'clock at night
I've seen the man who saw this wondrous sight.

Grand Papa *always* sends us something interesting in his letters.

There's something else about Grand Papa. He *loves* to keep lists: lists of how much money he spends every day; lists of the temperature on the thermometer, every morning, all year long; lists of the stars and planets he's seen with his telescope; lists of how many inches it rains; lists of the days when different flowers come out; lists of the birds he hears singing, and the date;

lists of the books he reads; lists of the letters he's sent and sends; list of the vegetables sold in the market. Lists, lists, lists!

Mama says Grand Papa was *always* like that. He was like that years ago, even before Grand Mama died, when Mama and Aunt Polly were just little old girls.

Here's a letter Grand Papa wrote from New York to poor Aunt Polly, fifteen years ago, when Aunt Polly was only twelve years old:

June 13, 1790

My dear Polly—

We had not peas nor strawberries here till the 8th day of this month. On the same day I heard the first whippoorwill whistle. Swallows and martins appeared here on the 21st of April. When did they appear with you? And when had you peas, strawberries, and whippoorwills in Virginia? Take notice, hereafter, whether the whippoorwills always come with the strawberries and peas. Send me a copy of the maxims I gave you. And a list of the books I promised you. When I come to Virginia I shall insist on eating a pudding of your own making.

Yours affectionately,
Th. Jefferson

Grand Papa loves to be busy. I've heard him say: "I'm as busy as a bee in a molasses barrel."

Mama says Grand Papa told her: "It is won-

derful how much may be done, if we are always doing."

Mama read Sister Anne and me part of another letter that Grand Papa wrote Aunt Polly, that same year, from New York:

April 11, 1790

My dear Polly—

How do you do? How are you occupied? Write me a letter by the first post and answer me all these questions:

Tell me whether you see the sun rise every day?

[Grand Papa loves to have everybody up and stirring, early in the morning. He says the sun hasn't caught him in bed for more than fifty years.]

How many pages a day you read in *Don Quixote*?

[That's Grand Papa's favorite book, I reckon. Aunt Polly was reading it, in *Spanish*!]

What else you read?
How many hours a day you sew?
Whether you continue your music?
Whether you know how to make a pudding yet?
To cut out a beef steak?
To sow spinach?
To set a hen?
Be good, my dear, as I have always found you.

Never be angry with anybody, nor speak harm of them.
Try to let everybody's faults be forgotten, as you would wish yours to be.
Take more pleasure in giving what is best to another, than in having it yourself.
Then, all the world will love you;

                    and I, more than all the world.
                    Th. Jefferson

So you can see that Grand Papa expects a great deal from all his family. And nowadays, from Jeff, and Sister Anne, and especially from *me*, *Ellen Aroon!*

He's always asking us things like: When did we have our first broiled shad in the spring? When did the willows first come into leaf? When did the strawberries first get ripe? Or the cherries, or the cucumbers, or the Indian corn, or the raspberries, or the peaches, or the cauliflower, or *something!*

Grand Papa says he's going to send me another pair of Bantams—a rooster and a hen—so I can raise some more chicks myself.

And if you can keep a secret, I'll tell you something else. Mama's going to have another baby! And we're all going to Washington City, again, this winter, to visit Grand Papa!

15

❧ 2 ❧

In Washington City

Washington City is just a tiny town. Grand Papa says there aren't but 3,210 people living here. The streets are muddy. Grand Papa had some poplar trees planted along Pennsylvania Avenue, but they're still just tiny.

Only part of the Capitol is finished. And the President's House isn't finished either. Some of the rooms don't have any plaster on the ceilings. Mama says it's a big drafty barn.

Grand Papa says it's big enough for "two emperors, one pope, and the grand lama in the bargain." There aren't any stone steps up to the front door yet. You have to walk up a wooden ramp to get to the entrance hall.

At the Capitol, the Senate chamber is built.

But the other Congressmen—the Representatives —don't have a regular meeting place yet. They meet in a sort of half-finished round brick building tacked onto the Capitol. It's so hot in there, most of the time, the Feds call it "the Dutch oven."

Grand Papa and Papa were mighty glad to see Mama and all of us children. Grand Papa has a steward here who's a Frenchman, named Etienne Lemaire. He lets us have pancakes for breakfast. Guess how he spells pancakes? *Panne-quaiques!* (That's because he's French!)

Sometimes Grand Papa has to have big dinners at night for the ambassadors from England and France and Spain. Mama says Grand Papa has three rules at his table:

1. No healths.
2. No politics.
3. No restraint.

He doesn't want any healths, because the ambassadors might drink too much wine, toasting each other. He doesn't want any politics, because he hates arguments. And he doesn't want any restraint, because he loves people to be free. He doesn't want waiters listening to what the guests

18

say. So, after they've served the dinner, Grand Papa makes them go away. Then he asks Jeff to come and pour the wine for everybody.

Jeff says Grand Papa has *Indians* to dinner, sometimes; Indians from way out west. Jeff says Grand Papa would much rather talk to the Indians than to the British Ambassador.

Here's the name of the British Ambassador: Mr. Merry. Here's what Grand Papa calls England: "the whale of the ocean." Here's what Grand Papa calls the United States: "the world's best hope." Here's what he calls the Indians: "my children." And here's what he calls being President: "splendid misery."

Mama says Grand Papa never smokes, or swears, or plays cards, or gambles. He never fights duels. He's always humming a tune, or telling jokes. Mama says he loves privacy and good manners. She says the psalm he loves best in the Bible is number twenty-five. And here's what he loves to say: "Be just, be true, love your neighbor as yourself, and your country more than yourself."

Mama says Grand Papa never contradicts anybody. That's something he learned from Dr. Benjamin Franklin, and Grand Papa says Dr.

Franklin was the most amiable man he ever knew.

Here's another thing Grand Papa won't ever do: he won't ever talk about his religion with anybody! He says his religious opinions are his own business, and he doesn't think the President should favor any one religion. That's why Grand Papa won't declare days of thanksgiving. He says the President shouldn't mix himself up in other people's religion. He won't even talk to *me* about religion!

Mama says Grand Papa never made any campaign speeches to get himself elected. He hates making all kinds of speeches, just like he hates arguing.

Jeff says one night, when Grand Papa had a big dinner, the Dutch Ambassador was there. Everybody helped themselves to a spoonful of sticky white pudding. Then the Dutch Ambassador dropped his napkin. When he leaned down to pick it up, by accident, his chin whiskers went into the pudding on his plate! Jeff heard the poor man whisper, "I vish I vass dead!" (I reckon he was embarrassed!)

Another time, Jeff went out for a drive in Grand Papa's carriage. He asked the driver to take him to the navy yard. Jeff wanted to see the ships. But you know what happened? The man in charge of the navy yard made all the sailors line up while Jeff went past and inspected them! Mama was angry with Jeff, for showing off. Grand Papa made Jeff go back to the navy yard and apologize. But, just the same, I don't think he thought Jeff had been all that naughty.

You know who Grand Papa hates? Napoleon. He's the emperor of the French. Grand Papa says Napoleon wants to rule the whole world. Grand Papa calls Napoleon "a most determined villain." Here's something else Grand Papa calls Napoleon: a tyrant. A tyrant is a cruel ruler who wants everything his own way. Grand Papa hates all tyrants. He has something stamped into the seal he seals his letters with. It says: "Rebellion to tyrants is obedience to God." (Mama says Grand Papa first heard that from Dr. Benjamin Franklin. She says it means that God doesn't think people should obey tyrants.)

Mama says Napoleon used to own a great big chunk of land, called Louisiana, right next to our country. But three years ago, Mama says, Grand Papa started trying to buy the whole parcel. So he sent a friend of his—Mr. James Monroe—over to France to talk to Napoleon.

Here's what Louisiana looks like. Grand Papa showed it to me on the map. See how big it is? Mama says it's bigger than the Union itself. When Mr. Monroe bought it for him, Grand Papa *doubled* the size of our country! And he didn't need any extra taxes to do it. And he didn't go to war for it, either!

Mama made me figure it out in an arithmetic lesson. Here's how much Grand Papa had to pay for Louisiana: $15,000,000. And here's what he got for the money: 1,171,931 square miles of land. I had to figure out how much Grand Papa had to pay for *one* square mile of land. You know what you do? You have to divide. Here's what it looks like:

$$
\begin{array}{r}
12.79 \\
1{,}171{,}931 \overline{)15{,}000{,}000.00} \\
11\ 719\ 31 \\
\hline
3\ 280\ 690 \\
2\ 343\ 862 \\
\hline
936\ 828\ 0 \\
820\ 351\ 7 \\
\hline
116\ 476\ 30 \\
105\ 473\ 79 \\
\hline
11\ 002\ 51
\end{array}
$$

Mama says *that* means that Louisiana cost Grand Papa about $12.80 per square mile. She says

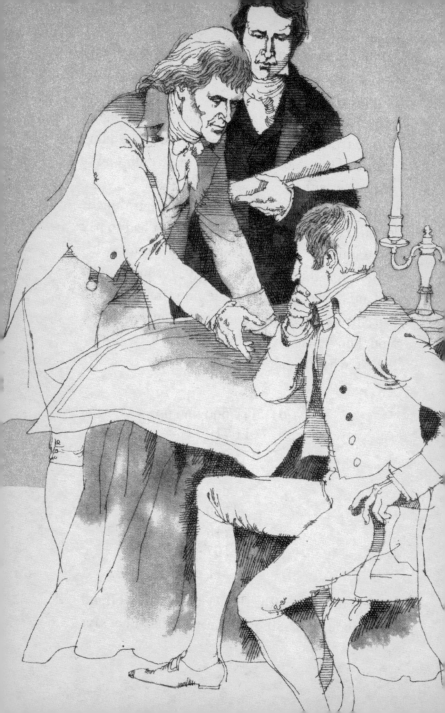

that's quite a good bargain! Of course Grand Papa is still just *guessing* at how much land is out there. Nobody knows for sure. Nobody knows how far it stretches, or just who lives there.

Grand Papa says there may be woolly mammoths, or even dinosaurs, still living out there! He says somewhere in it, it may have a huge mountain of salt!

The Feds laugh at Grand Papa. They say, "Isn't that just like Mr. Mammoth? Next thing he'll be telling us there's a valley full of corn pudding way up the Missouri River! And a great big lake of molasses!"

But Grand Papa doesn't care how much the Feds laugh at him. He's sent Meriwether Lewis (who used to be his private secretary) and William Clark, and some soldiers and trappers out there to see what they can see. He wants them to go all the way up the Missouri River, and clear on out to the Pacific Ocean, if they can!

Since I've been in Washington City I've met Mrs. Margaret Smith. She's a pretty lady. Her husband owns a newspaper here. She's not a Fed. She was nice to me and had me to her house for a whole day. She read me lots of poems, and she told Mama I'm real intelligent.

I've gotten to know Mrs. Dolley Madison, too. Dolley Madison is married to short, little old James Madison. Mr. Madison is one of Grand Papa's best friends. He's Grand Papa's Secretary of State, and helps him run things in Washington City.

I like Dolley Madison. When she sees Sister Anne dressed up to go to parties and balls, she tells Mama how beautiful Sister Anne looks. But she tells Mama how *smart* I am!

Mama wanted some nice things to wear in Washington City, so here's what Dolley Madison brought her from Baltimore: some combs for her hair, a new bonnet, a shawl, a wig, and a white lace veil.

Dolley Madison told me how Grand Papa made Mr. Merry, the British Ambassador, angry. When Mr. Merry came to the President's House to shake hands with Grand Papa for the first time, he was all dressed up. But Grand Papa was wearing his old red carpet slippers. (Mama says Grand Papa doesn't like the British so much, and besides, he thinks dressing up is a heap of foolishness.) Dolley Madison said Mr. Merry got red in the face, he was so angry! And then she laughed and laughed.

Dolley Madison told me how it was when Grand Papa first came in, as President, way back on March 4, 1801. She told me about the parade they had, in Philadelphia, for Grand Papa. There were only sixteen states then. Now there are seventeen. Do you know the name of the seventeenth? Here it is: Ohio. In the parade there were sixteen white horses hitched to a carriage. One horse for every state of the Union. And set on top of the carriage was a big ship of state with sails set and flags flying. It was called the *Thomas Jefferson*. And people shot off cannons and cheered.

And Dolley Madison told me how all kinds of Indian chiefs come here to talk to Grand Papa when he has his Galas on the Fourth of July and on New Year's Day. A Gala is a big party. Grand Papa won't have any parties any other time *but* New Year's Day and the Fourth of July.

Grand Papa thought the Feds used to have too many fancy parties for their own good, when *they* were running things. People ask Grand Papa to let them give him a party on his birthday. But Grand Papa says no. He won't even let people know when his birthday is. But Dolley Madison and I know what day it is. It's April 13.

I told Dolley Madison that Grand Papa was spending too much money as President. Last year he spent $33,000, and that's $8,000 more than his salary!

Dolley Madison laughed. "How do you know all about that, Ellen?" she asked.

I told her I heard Grand Papa telling Papa about it. And Dolley Madison just laughed some more.

Grand Papa told me that one year some farmers from Massachusetts made him a present of a great big enormous cheese. It was four feet wide, and it weighed 1,235 pounds. That's more than half a ton! But Grand Papa wouldn't take it as a gift. He paid the men $200 for it. Grand Papa doesn't believe in taking presents while he's President.

Yesterday Grand Papa let me eat a new dessert made by his French cook. Nobody in this country has ever tasted it before. It's called ice cream.

Guess what happened to Mama while we've been visiting Grand Papa? She had her new baby! It's a little boy. Grand Papa says we're going to call him James Madison Randolph, after Mr. Madison. Dolley Madison was *so pleased*! My little brother is the first baby ever to be born in the President's House! Little old James

Madison Randolph! Grand Papa calls him "Patsy's new bantling."

And now I have to tell you about Dick. Dick is Grand Papa's pet mockingbird. Grand Papa keeps him in a cage in his study. Lots of times he lets Dick out of his cage. Dick sits on Grand Papa's books and sings and sings. He eats seeds out of Grand Papa's hands. He perches on Grand Papa's shoulder. He flies around from chair to chair. Grand Papa loves mockingbirds. I don't know what he'd do without Dick. Grand Papa once told me and Sister Anne and Jeff and Cornelia and Virginia and Mary that if we *ever* harmed a mockingbird, or stole eggs from its nest, the mockingbirds would come back and haunt us! And Mama says it's true!

❦ 3 ❦

At Monticello

We're all back home at Edgehill. Even Papa is here. Papa's full name is Thomas Mann Randolph. He's part Indian. He has dark hair. He's descended from Pocahontas.

Later on this summer Grand Papa will come to Virginia, too. Here's the first thing Grand Papa does when he comes to Edgehill. He carries every single one of us over to *his* house, Monticello, to be with him all summer long; Mama and Papa, Sister Anne and Jeff, Cornelia, Virginia, Mary, baby James Madison, and me, Ellen Aroon! Grand Papa wants all of us with him, Uncle Jack Eppes and Francis and Maria, and all of our aunts and uncles and cousins. He wants his whole family to be with him at Monticello.

You can see Monticello from Edgehill. It's way up on top of a mountain, about four or five miles away. Grand Papa says its name means "Little Mountain," in Italian. Grand Papa named it, and found the mountain he wanted to build it on, and drew the plans for the house all by himself.

Mama says Grand Papa is a fine architect. There's no other house quite like it in Virginia, or in the whole world. From way up there, you can look in every direction for miles and miles. Most people want their houses to look bigger than they really are, but Grand Papa designed Monticello to look *smaller* than it really is. Monticello really has three stories, but Grand Papa designed it to look as if it hadn't got but one! Isn't that *just* like Grand Papa? He thinks Monticello is the loveliest spot on earth. So does Mama. And so do I.

Here's one reason Monticello is so beautiful: its gardens. I think Grand Papa would rather spend his time gardening than anything else in the world—except reading, maybe, or writing letters. Grand Papa says he likes farmers better than any other kinds of men on earth.

Grand Papa orders plants and shrubs and trees from all over the world for this hilltop. They

come from France and Italy and China and Spain. He has every kind of tree you can think of: flowering trees, shade trees, evergreen trees, nut trees, fruit trees. He grows walnuts and pecans, chestnuts, hickory nuts, and butternuts, apples, pears, and strawberries, and grapes and plums, raspberries and currants, persimmons and figs, and peaches, watermelons, and nectarines. His gardeners, Wormley and Goliath, grow celery and radishes, asparagus and lettuce, cauliflower and onions, carrots and beets, corn and squash, broccoli, spinach, and beans. And they grow Grand Papa's favorite vegetable, green peas.

I quit counting how many different kinds of peas there were, after I counted nineteen! Peas are one of the first vegetables to get ripe for the table in spring. Do you know what Grand Papa does when his very first mess of garden peas are ready to eat in the springtime? He asks all his neighbors to come to dinner, to help him celebrate.

One time, when the peas came in, Grand Papa asked Mr. and Mrs. Madison to come to dinner. Mr. Madison likes to lean back in his chair at the table, and he was sitting in front of an open window that goes right down to the floor. Mr.

Madison likes to imitate politicians. He was imitating Patrick Henry.

"Here's what Patrick Henry says about Mr. Jefferson," said Mr. Madison. "He says Mr. Jefferson eats so much fine French cooking, he's quit eatin' all his favorite Virginia foods. No more ham! No more cornbread! He has abjured his native vittles!" And Mr. Madison commenced laughing so hard, he fell backwards, right out of the window onto the lawn!

The next day, Grand Papa told Heming, the carpenter, to put railings on all those windows.

Sister Anne knows more about flowers than I do, so she helps Grand Papa with them. He and Sister Anne grow tulips and narcissus, roses and hollyhocks, larkspur and lilies of the valley, violets and daffodils, hyacinths and tuberoses, daisies and buttercups, poppies and peonies, lilacs and orange blossoms, camellias and jasmine. There's something sweet-smelling all year long.

Some flowers have very fancy names, especially the tulips. Grand Papa told Sister Anne there's a beautiful white tulip called Marcus Aurelius; and there's a beautiful red tulip called Queen of the Amazons. I just wish you could see how Sister Anne carries on, in springtime, when the tulips get ready to bloom.

40

"Oh, Grand Papa!" she calls. "Come quick! Come look! The Queen of the Amazons is blooming!" Now isn't that *just* like Sister Anne?

Sometimes, at Monticello, we go say hello to Mr. Bacon. He's the overseer. And there's Davy, who drives the wagons with his mules. The mules are named Dolphin, and Captain Molly, and Doll Tweezer, and Rinctum, and Dr. Slop. Davy carries fresh vegetables and fruit to Grand Papa in Washington City. Then Davy brings back seeds and bulbs, trees, shrubs, and geraniums to plant at Monticello.

At Monticello, you have to walk through a long, stone underground tunnel to get to the kitchen. The kitchen isn't part of the main house. That's so if it catches on fire, the whole house won't burn down. It's the same kitchen where old Aunt Ursula used to bake her cakes. Before she died, my Grand Mama used to come down here to read recipes out loud to Ursula, because Ursula couldn't read. Ursula's husband used to be Grand Papa's coachman. His name was King George. Sometimes they called Ursula, "Queenie." Aunt Ursula died when I was four years old. Mama used to call her "Mammy." Aunt Ursula used to switch Mama and Aunt

Polly with a peach switch, when they were naughty.

Then there's Uncle Isaac. He works at Monticello. He's another one of Grand Papa's slaves. Uncle Isaac remembers the Revolution. He told me about the time—when he was just a little boy about seven—when the British cavalry rode up the mountain to Monticello, trying to capture Grand Papa. Grand Papa knew they were coming, so he could ride away in plenty of time. But Isaac stayed behind, here, to help bury the silverware under the porch. The British never got hold of it. But Isaac says the British soldiers drank up all of Grand Papa's wine.

Do you know why the British wanted to catch Grand Papa? They were angry with him. It was because of a letter he wrote to their king, King George III. Mama says *he* was a tyrant, too! What Grand Papa wrote was not a letter, really. It was more like an *announcement*. What Grand Papa wrote in it was that from now on everybody in America was going to be free. It was called the Declaration of Independence. Grand Papa showed me the little writing desk he wrote it on. He had the desk made in Philadelphia. It's in his library.

Mama says Grand Papa finished writing the

Declaration of Independence on July 4, 1776. Mama says that's why we have barbecues and fireworks every year on this day. If it wasn't for Grand Papa, we wouldn't have any reason at all to celebrate the Fourth of July!

Mama got a letter from Grand Papa today. Guess what's happened? He's heard from Lewis and Clark—the men he sent out to explore Louisiana. They're safe! They'll be coming home! They traveled thousands and thousands of miles. They got to the headwaters of the Missouri River. They found the place where it splits up into three rivers. And they named the three streams the Gallatin (for Mr. Albert Gallatin—that's Grand Papa's Secretary of the Treasury), the Madison (that's for Mr. Madison), and the Jefferson, for Grand Papa!

Mama says Meriwether Lewis and William Clark got to the Pacific Ocean. An Indian girl, named Sacajawea, helped them find horses so they could cross the mountains. And they're going to send some Indians to Washington City to meet Grand Papa.

Here's what Grand Papa told Mama he was sending to Monticello: some plants and some minerals they found, a buffalo robe painted by the Indians, the antlers of a moose and an elk, and the hide of a great big grizzly bear. And some Indian pipes and hatchets and robes, some live magpies and a live prairie dog, a map of the Missouri River, and some of the words the Indians use . . . and some *mammoth bones*!

Now let the Feds try to laugh at Mr. Mammoth, if they can!

And Grand Papa's going to put all that rigamarole of stuff right here, in the hall, at Monticello. Mama said, "My goodness, what will Papa think of next?"

And you know what happened after that? Grand Papa came from Washington City, home to Virginia, for his summer vacation. First he rode to Edgehill on his favorite horse, Castor. Castor is a bay. (A bay is a reddish-brown horse.) He came real early in the morning and he crept upstairs, and he *caught me in bed!* I was fast asleep!

"Ellen Aroon!" said Grand Papa. "You're a sleepy-head. And I've caught you in bed again!"

Sister Anne told Grand Papa she *knew* he'd catch me in bed. She says I'm lazy, and I take too long dressing. But Mama and Grand Papa just laughed, and we all went downstairs for a breakfast of biscuits and jam.

Mama asked Grand Papa if he'd remembered to bring her the coffee cups. "I'll need them for the summer visitations," said Mama. She means all the visitors who come to see Grand Papa at Monticello in summer.

Sometimes Mama has to feed *fifty* people for dinner. Mr. Bacon says the visitors eat up all the hams in the smokehouses, and their horses eat up all the hay in the barns. But Grand Papa never turns strangers away, not if they have letters from friends of his. (But Grand Papa didn't much like that strange lady who punched a piece of glass out of his hall window with her umbrella, just so she could get a better look at him!) Sometimes the visitors stay for weeks and weeks. Grand Papa doesn't seem to mind.

Here's how Grand Papa spends his day resting at Monticello. He gets up at daybreak. If it's chilly his servant, Burwell, makes him a fire in the fireplace. Then Grand Papa reads, or writes letters before breakfast. Grand Papa has a machine in his study that makes a second copy of his letters while he writes them! It's called a polygraph.

Grand Papa has a leather chair that swivels around and around. He invented it himself. He

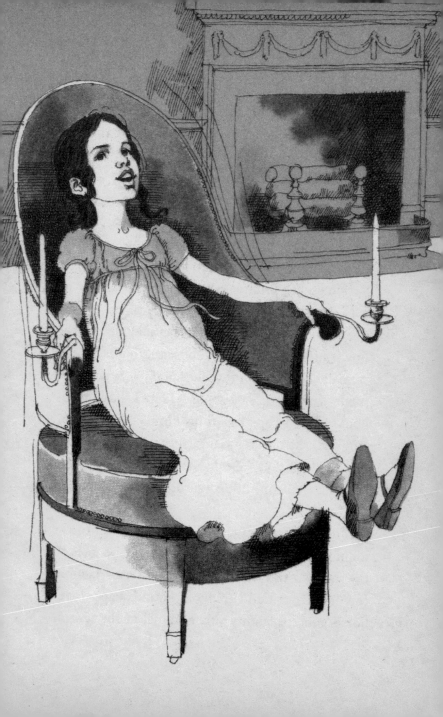

lets me turn around and around on it whenever I want.

"Grand Papa," I said, "it spins around just like a top or a whirligig." (A whirligig is a toy, and you blow in at one end of a hollow tube, and then a little paddle wheel at the other end spins around in the jet of air.)

"It *does* spin around like a whirligig, Ellen Aroon," said Grand Papa. "And that's just what the Feds have called it. Mr. Jefferson's *whirligig chair*!" And we have a good laugh at the Feds.

Sometimes Grand Papa reads in his study before breakfast. When Grand Papa is looking something up in his books, he sometimes takes down fifteen or twenty books at a time. Then he spreads them out on the floor and paces back and forth, from book to book. Here's how many books Grand Papa has in his library: 9,000. And here's all the different languages that Grand Papa can read: Latin, Greek, Anglo-Saxon, French, Spanish, Italian, and *English*! (I can read *that* one, too!)

Then Grand Papa goes to breakfast in the dining room. And then, around nine, he goes to the stables. And they saddle up Castor or Jacobin for him to ride. I reckon Grand Papa loves horses more than any other animal in the world.

He goes for long, long rides down by the river to see his mill, and he rides over his fields. Grand Papa looks over his crops for hours and hours, and doesn't come home until dinnertime, at three in the afternoon. He says maybe Sister Anne and I can ride with him, when we're older.

When there's company at dinner, sometimes we don't get up from the table until five o'clock. But before the sun goes down, we children go walking with Grand Papa. Sometimes we go look at the trout in the trout pond. Sometimes we run races on the lawn, and Grand Papa pulls cherries down, from the trees, using a hook on the end of a stick, to give a prize to the winner!

And then when the sun goes down, Burwell and Critta and Bet bring candles to be lit, and sometimes we read until bedtime. And sometimes Grand Papa plays games with us for an hour.

Sometimes, at sunset, we sit on the portico, watching the sun go down over the Blue Ridge Mountains. When Grand Papa looks up at the ceiling, the inside weathervane, there, tells him which way the wind is blowing outdoors.

But tonight, when it gets dark enough, Grand Papa is going to take us up to the top of the house, into the dome, and let us look through his telescope. He's going to show us the rings of

Saturn. Saturn is a planet, and it has these pretty golden bands, or rings, around it.

Right now, we're waiting for it to get good and dark. All of us children are playing a game with Grand Papa. It's a game he likes a lot. It's called "I Love My Love." Grand Papa taught it to us. It goes like this.

Sister Anne and Cornelia and Virginia and Grand Papa and Mama and I sit in circle on the portico. Anne begins with A. "I love my love with an A. His name is Arthur. He lives in Albany. He drinks ale and eats apples. He is an acrobat. And he loves . . . alligators!" Everything has to begin with an A! See?

And now Virginia goes, with B. "I love my love with a B. His name is Bruce. He lives in Boston. He drinks beer and eats beans. He works in a bakery. And he likes . . . bees!"

Now it's *my* turn. "I love my love with a C. His name is Conrad. He lives in China. He drinks coffee and eats cookies. He is a carpenter. And he likes . . . cats!"

Then comes Cornelia. "I love my love with a D. His name is Donald. He lives in Danbury. He drinks . . . dew! And he eats dumplings. And he loves dogs!"

And then comes Grand Papa. He looks at me and smiles. "I love my love," he says, "with an E. Her name is Ellen Aroon. She lives at Edgehill. She drinks elderberry wine. And she eats eggs, and endive, and *eels*!"

"Oh, Grand Papa!" squeals Sister Anne. Isn't that *just* like Sister Anne?

Grand Papa goes right on. "She is exceptionally eager, energetic, endearing, engaging, elegant, exotic, *and* enchanting! And she loves . . . *everybody*!"

"Oh, Papa!" says Mama. "You're going to spoil that child."

But by now it's dark enough for all of us to go up into the dome, and look at the rings of Saturn. We all stand there quietly while Grand Papa focuses the lens of his telescope. Then at last he says, "There she is!" and he lets me be the first to look. They look so pretty I just forget everything Mama ever told me, and I say: "They're mighty pretty, Mr. Mammoth!"

And Grand Papa looks at me, real deep into my eyes and we both begin to laugh. Grand Papa is still laughing when he takes me up to bed and kisses me good night. "Yes, mighty pretty," says Grand Papa. "Mighty pretty, Ellen Aroon!"

Thomas Jefferson (April 13, 1743–July 4, 1826) accomplished so much that he seems to have lived fifteen or twenty lifetimes in the space of his eighty-three years. In 1776, he wrote the Declaration of Independence; he later became Governor of Virginia; from 1783 to 1789, he was our ambassador to France; in 1790, he became Secretary of State for President Washington; in 1796, he was Vice-President under John Adams; from 1801 to 1809, he was President of the United States—during which administration he purchased the vast territory of Louisiana, which gave the United States more land than Napoleon ever conquered; and in the last years of his life, he founded the University of Virginia. In addition to all this, he read thousands of books, wrote thousands and thousands of letters, and found time for gardening, writing, inventions, science, architecture, music, astronomy, and a rich life with his daughters' families, his relatives, and his friends. They were achievements worthy of his nickname, "Mr. Mammoth."

His wife, Martha Wayles Jefferson, died in 1782, after having been married to him for ten years, leaving three children: Martha ("Patsy"); Mary ("Maria," or "Polly"); and Lucy Elizabeth. Lucy (aged two years) died of whooping cough in 1784, while her father was in France. Patsy and Polly grew to womanhood—Patsy marrying Thomas Mann Randolph, and Polly marrying John Wayles Eppes.

Polly (Maria Jefferson Eppes) had only one child who lived into adulthood—her son, Francis Wayles Eppes (1801–81). Her daughter, Maria Jefferson Eppes, died in 1807, at age three. And Polly herself (1778–1804) died young, in her twenty-sixth year.

But Patsy (Martha Jefferson Randolph) had eleven children, all of whom grew up to delight their adoring Grand Papa. It is simplest just to list them:

Anne Cary Randolph (1791–1826)
Thomas Jefferson Randolph (1792–1875)
Ellen Wayles Randolph (1796–1876)
Cornelia Jefferson Randolph (1799–1871)
Virginia Jefferson Randolph (1801–1882)
Mary Jefferson Randolph (1803–1876)
James Madison Randolph (1806–1834)

Benjamin Franklin Randolph (1808–1871)
Meriwether Lewis Randolph (1810–1837)
Septimia Anne Randolph (1814–1887)
George Wythe Randolph (1818–1867)

This story, of course, tells just a few of the events of the years from 1805 to 1806, which "Ellen Aroon" (Ellen Wayles Randolph) could have observed as a child of nine or ten.

Ellen was probably Jefferson's favorite granddaughter, and he and she were devoted to one another all their lives.

Jefferson died on July 4, 1826, exactly fifty years—to the day —after the signing of the Declaration of Independence. But about a year before that, Ellen married (May 27, 1825) Joseph Coolidge, of Boston, a merchant in the China trade. The ship carrying Ellen's wedding presents (but fortunately not the bride and groom), from Virginia to Boston, was lost at sea. Among the sunken treasures was a beautifully inlaid desk which John Hemings (the Monticello carpenter and old Negro slave) had carved for Ellen. John was too old and his eyesight too dim for him to make her another. "Everything else seemed as nothing in his eye," wrote Jefferson to Ellen, in November, "and that loss was everything. Virgil could not have been more afflicted had his *Aeneid* fallen a prey to the flames."

Jefferson decided to send Ellen a "substitute, not claiming the same value from its decorations, but from the part it has borne in our history. . . ." "For surely," he wrote, "a connection with the great Charter of our Independence may give a value to what has been associated with that. . . . Now I happen still to possess the writing box on which it [the Declaration of Independence] was written. It was made from a drawing of my own by Benjamin Randolph, a cabinetmaker in whose house I took my first lodgings on my arrival in Philadelphia in May, 1776. And I have used it ever since. It claims no merit of particular beauty. It is plain, neat, convenient, and taking no more room on the writing table than a moderate quarto volume, it yet displays itself sufficiently for any writing. Mr. Coolidge must do me the favor of accepting this. Its imaginary value will increase with the years, and if he lives to my age [82] or another half century, he may see it carried in the procession of our nation's birthday, as the relics of the saints are in those of the church."

Ellen kept the writing desk all her life, and it may now be seen in the National Museum, in Washington, D.C.

The Coolidges had six children—two girls and four boys. Their youngest son was named Thomas Jefferson Coolidge, after Ellen's Grand Papa. And another of her sons, Sydney, was killed in 1863, during the Civil War, fighting for the Union.

By a strange turn of fate, Ellen's youngest brother, George Wythe Randolph, was on the side of the Confederacy, and served for a time as Jefferson Davis's Secretary of War.

Ellen and Joseph Coolidge were happily married for fifty-two years. Ellen died in 1876; her husband, three years later.

By way of his many grandchildren and great-grandchildren, Thomas Jefferson has thousands and thousands of direct descendants living in America today. And in a larger sense, he is the Grand Papa of all who love liberty, all over the world.

A final word about Jefferson and slavery: he recognized slavery to be one of the greatest evils of his times, but—like every other statesman in America in his era—could find no way to eradicate it completely, without being willing to resort to war. He did manage to have slavery prohibited in the Northwest Territory (the lands that were later to become the states of Ohio, Indiana, Illinois, etc.), but was distressed to see his condemnation of slavery struck from his original draft of the Declaration of Independence (at the insistence of South Carolina and Georgia).

In his will, he was able to free a few of his own personal slaves (he owned about 150), but since virtually all of his property (including his slaves) was mortgaged, and since he was overwhelmed by debt, it was impossible for him to free the great majority of them.

I should like to thank Sylvia C. Hilton and the staff of the New York Society Library (where most of the research for this book was done), for their unfailing assistance to me; and also Roger Lea MacBride for permitting me to visit "Esmont" (a home quite possibly designed by Jefferson himself); Ray Graham, for allowing me to explore the former Randolph place, "Edgehill"; and James A. Bear, Jr., Curator of the Thomas Jefferson Memorial Foundation in Charlottesville, Virginia, for his kindness in showing me rooms in the upper stories of Monticello not ordinarily on view to the public. F. N. M.

BIBLIOGRAPHY

Andrist, Ralph K., and Bingham, E. R. *To the Pacific with Lewis & Clark*. New York: Harper & Row, American Heritage Junior Library, 1967.

Bear, James Adam Jr., ed. *Jefferson at Monticello*. Charlottesville: University Press of Virginia, 1967.

Betts, Edwin M., and Bear, James Adam Jr. *The Family Letters of Thomas Jefferson*. Columbia: University of Missouri Press, 1966.

Betts, Edwin M., and Perkins, Hazlehurst B. *Thomas Jefferson's Flower Garden at Monticello*. Charlottesville: University Press of Virginia, 1971.

Boykin, Edward. *To the Girls and Boys*. New York: Funk & Wagnalls, 1964.

Dillon, Richard. *Meriwether Lewis*. New York: Coward-McCann, 1965.

Hall, Gordon Langley. *Mr. Jefferson's Ladies*. Boston: Beacon Press, 1966.

Lipscomb, A. A., and Bergh, E. A. E. *The Writings of Thomas Jefferson*. Washington, D.C.: Thomas Jefferson Memorial Association, 1904.

Moscow, Henry. *Thomas Jefferson and His World*. New York: Harper & Row, American Heritage Junior Library, 1960.

Nichols, F. D., and Bear, James Adam Jr. *Monticello*, Monticello: Thomas Jefferson Memorial Foundation, 1967.

Padover, Saul K. *Jefferson*. New York: Harcourt, Brace & Co., 1942. rev & abr ed New York: New American Library, 1952.

Parton, James. *Life of Thomas Jefferson*. 1874. Reprint (American Scene Series). New York: Plenum Publishing Corporation, 1971.

Randall, Henry S. *The Life of Thomas Jefferson*. 3 vols. 1858. Reprint (American Scene Series). New York: Plenum Publishing Corporation, 1964.

Randolph, Sarah N. *The Domestic Life of Thomas Jefferson*. New York: Harper & Brothers, 1871.

Shackleford, G. G., ed. *Collected Papers of the Descendants of Thomas Jefferson*. Princeton: Princeton University Press, 1965.